You Can Always Find A Way

Written & Illustrated by Natalie Lawrence Rush

ISBN 978-0-578-85731-2

Book design by Gabriel Enck

This book is dedicated to my daughters: Sophia & Sarah,
and their friends: Isabella & Sofia
(who inspired this story)

Also, in loving memory of my father:

Robert S. Lawrence

Thank you:

A special thank you to Elizabeth, Eddie, and our girls for your friendship in order to help make this dream of publishing a book possible.

Much thanks to my husband Greg, nephew Gabe, sister-in-law Melissa, and Amy J. for helping to edit and review. I am truly grateful for the support of all my family, friends, and colleagues.

It was the first day of second grade, and Grace was feeling very nervous. Her teacher was Mr. Simon, and it was the first time she had a male teacher – not to mention the fact that Grace didn't know anyone in her class.

The next day, Grace noticed a girl from class was at her bus stop. "I wonder why I haven't seen her at the bus stop until now," Grace thought. Grace sat down next to the new girl on the bus. "Hi, I'm Grace. You're in Mr. Simon's class, right?" she asked.

"Oh hi! Yes, my name is Ella," she said with a smile.

"Did you just move here?" asked Grace.

"Yes," Ella replied. "My dad is in the military, so we move around a lot," she said. Grace and Ella began to talk more and more...

They sat together at lunch, played at recess, and rode with one another on the bus each day.

When Halloween came, the girls went trick-or-treating with each other in their neighborhood. Grace introduced her mom to Ella's mom, and they exchanged numbers to set up a playdate.

That night, Ella's little sister, Emma, met Grace's little sister, Rose, who were about the same age. Grace, Ella, and their sisters had a blast trick-or-treating together!

Grace and Ella began to play after school, and on weekends, at each other's houses or the park.

Their little sisters, Rose and Emma, wanted to have playdates, too. So, if one sister went, then the other usually went along as well.

Both Emma and Rose played soccer. Sometimes, Grace and Ella would go to the soccer field to watch their little sisters' practice.

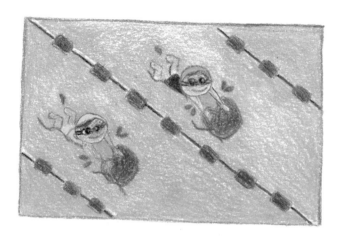

Grace and Ella soon learned that they
shared common interests such as
swimming and martial arts.

Grace even overcame her fear of dogs because Ella had two of them! Grace became very fond of Fluffy and Fifi.

As Grace and Ella's friendship grew,
so did Rose and Emma's.

Like their big sisters, they enjoyed playing make-believe and dress-up.

Before moving here, Ella hoped that her family would move to a place where she could see snow.

The weather started changing as fall turned to winter, and Ella got her wish!

The girls got to sled ride, make snow angels, throw snowballs, and build snowmen. Ella really enjoyed her first snow day!

As the girls' friendship grew, their moms also became good friends.

In springtime, they would picnic at the park. Sometimes, the girls would practice riding their bikes without training wheels!

They enjoyed visiting the local library,
where they borrowed books to read.

Kids' Chess Club
Wednesdays @ 5PM

Chess Club was an activity
the girls had fun doing together.

In the summertime, the girls' moms would take them swimming at the local pool where they all had a great time!

Grace's and Ella's families even
went camping together.

They took turns cooking and
made hot chocolate over the fire.

At night, the girls loved catching
fireflies! Ella's family hadn't seen
them before moving here.

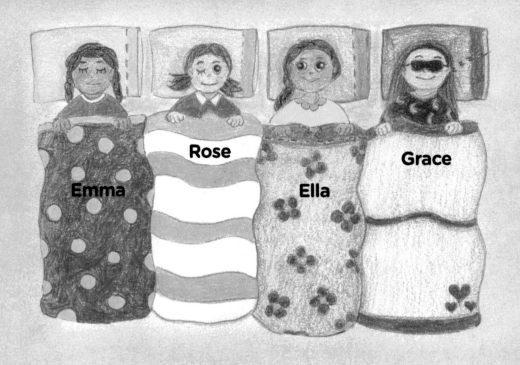

The girls slept in the same tent at camp. It was so much fun making memories and spending time with good friends!

As time passed, the friends became inseparable. Then, near the end of fourth grade, Grace knew it would be coming to an end. The military assigned Ella's dad a new job across the country, so they had to move.

The girls promised to keep in touch. Grace bought
"Best Friends" necklaces as a going away present for Ella.

Once Ella and Emma were on the road, they video-chatted,
and Ella sent postcards of their journey. The girls stayed
connected after Ella's family settled into their new home.

As fifth grade came, Grace really missed her best friend. The girls would mail presents to one another on special occasions, but school was just not the same.

When spring arrived, all Grace wanted for her birthday was to fly out west and see her best friend, Ella!

Once her parents agreed, it was all Grace could think and talk about!

Finally...